BITTERSWEET JOURNEY

BITTERSWEET JOURNEY

JOURNEY

A Modestly
Erotic Novel *of*
Love, Longing,
and Chocolate

Enid Futterman

Designed *by*
Alexander Isley Inc.

viking

VIKING

Published by the Penguin Group

Penguin Putnam Inc., 375 Hudson Street,
New York, New York 10014, U.S.A.
Penguin Books Ltd, 27 Wrights Lane,
London W8 5TZ, England
Penguin Books Australia Ltd, Ringwood,
Victoria, Australia
Penguin Books Canada Ltd, 10 Alcorn Avenue,
Toronto, Ontario, Canada M4V 3B2
Penguin Books (N.Z.) Ltd, 182–190 Wairau Road,
Auckland 10, New Zealand

Penguin Books Ltd, Registered Offices:
Harmondsworth, Middlesex, England

First published in 1998 by Viking Penguin,
a member of Penguin Putnam Inc.

1 3 5 7 9 10 8 6 4 2

Photographs by the author

LIBRARY OF CONGRESS CATALOGING IN PUBLICATION DATA
Futterman, Enid.
Bittersweet journey: a modestly erotic novel of love,
longing, and chocolate/Enid Futterman.
p. cm.
ISBN 0-670-87694-1
I. Title.
PS3556.U88B58   1998
813'.54—dc21   97-25202

This book is printed on acid-free paper.

∞

Printed in Singapore by Toppan Printing Co.
Set in Centaur
Designed by Alexander Isley Inc.

ACKNOWLEDGMENTS

To my agent, Martha Kaplan, for her wisdom, patience, and humor. To my
editors, Dawn Drzal and Wendy Wolf, for the intelligence and attention with which
they helped bring this book into being, and to Roni Axelrod, for having a vision
and fulfilling it. To Alex Isley, for framing my pictures and words with beauty, clarity,
and invention. And to Jim Walsh, president of Hawaiian Vintage Chocolate, for
his generosity in sharing his knowledge and his chocolate.

TO THE MEMORY OF RICHARD LEVENSON

who showed me how to see in the dark

One does not become enlightened
by imagining figures of light,
but by making the darkness
conscious.
—C. G. Jung

Once, in a dream land called Toilan,

there was a dream city called Tuila,

surrounded by a garden of *cahuaguahitl* trees,

planted by the King and tended by the Queen.

The King and Queen were beloved and worshiped,

as the God of Light, Quetzalcoatl,

and the Goddess of Love, Xochiquetzal.

I.

SEDUCTION

Candy

Kisses

BROOKLYN

Chapter I

Her father's kisses were candy bars, which her mother had forbidden.

Every evening at seven, Charlotte would hear his key in the lock and she would run to greet him. He would not lift her into his arms, but he would smile their secret smile before he removed his hat and coat and hung them in the closet in the hall.

She would wait until he had walked wearily down the hall and into the bathroom to wash his hands. Then she would open the closet and put her hand in the pocket of his heavy grey overcoat. She would smell it before she felt it, thin, flat, and hard. The words of her parents' sharp voices were garbled, but she could hear the round sound of her own heart beating. She would lift her treasure quickly from its hiding place, and hide it again, hoping her mother was too busy feeding, or finding fault with, her father to notice.

After supper, which she would pick at, after *I Remember Mama* or *Father Knows Best*, she would brush her teeth and hair, take off her school clothes, and put on her pajamas. She would turn off the light, climb under heavy blankets, reach under her pillow, and unwrap it slowly and quietly in the darkness. She would close her eyes and open her mouth.

It quieted and excited her at the same time. Everything about it was a relief—its flavor, color, fragrance, even its name, which was so like hers. Sometimes she would whisper it, like a magic word, as if by saying it, she could taste it. It was a word of consonants, a collision of hard and soft sounds. She would utter them slowly, savoring even the tiny silence between the two syllables, and the almost inaudible *t*.

Chocolate.

To Charlotte, a chocolate bar was a Hershey bar. Nothing else could provoke the same hopeful, fearful anticipation, or provide the same profound pleasure. And although it was milk chocolate (which, otherwise, she hated), it was darker; to the innocent palate of a child, it was almost bittersweet.

She loved its plainness; almonds would get in the way. She loved the glossy brown paper and the shiny silver letters that caught her eye in movie houses, grocery stores, and subway stations, long after she had grown up. She even loved the stories of American soldiers who gave Hershey bars to grateful French girls. Her father was her American hero, and she was his *jeune fille*. Until she turned twelve and entered that brief time in the life of a woman when she is, or believes herself to be, herself.

At twelve, she knew things, and could do things. Snap pictures with her own camera. Take the subway to Coney Island and ride a Steeplechase horse. Buy her own chocolate bars at the candy store around the corner.

At twelve, when her mother did not even cook, other mothers baked. Charlotte was not impressed by cakes, not even chocolate ones, or brownies. Too much cake; not enough chocolate. But when another mother made fudge, she was allowed to stir the bubbling brown mixture with a wooden spoon, tracing the shape of a figure eight on the bottom of the pot. The pot was a cauldron; the figure eight, a hex symbol.

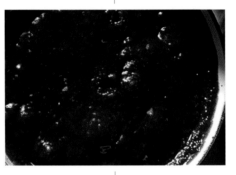

Her first taste of fudge came years before her first kiss, but it was just as sensational. A familiar, beloved taste was suffused with warmth and depth, and it stirred her in a completely new way, instilling the false hope that her own mother, who considered sugar poison, would make fudge too.

In the middle of that night, on her way to the bathroom, Charlotte saw a light, and in it, her mother, with a strange and sad expression on her face. Her book was lying, facedown, on the arm of the easy chair. Charlotte's gaze was as fixed as her mother's, until her eyes wandered to an open box of Barton's kosher bonbons. A relative had brought them for Passover, but they had disappeared faster than the *afikomen*. She returned to bed, angry but resolute. The other mother would teach her how to make fudge; she would give herself permission to eat it.

Shortly after her thirteenth birthday, the window that had opened began to close. The boys she wanted were not the boys who wanted her. She was baffled. Her father adored her; why didn't they? But her father left her every morning before she awoke, so that he could be in his office in New York at seven. "New York" was what people who lived in Brooklyn called Manhattan.

Long before she left home, she had forgotten how to make fudge, and had withdrawn the permission she had given herself to eat chocolate. She had become her own mother, and could no longer receive her father's kisses.

She would utter them slowly
savoring even the tiny silence between the
two syllables, and the almost inaudible t.

chocolate

NET WT.
1.55 OZ
(43 g)

NEW YORK

Chapter 2

To a child of Brooklyn, Manhattan is the Empire State Building, Radio City Music Hall, and Macy's.

Even after she had a New York job (as a photographer's assistant) and a tiny New York apartment, Charlotte yearned for New York. It did not welcome, especially in winter, when the nights came before the days were done, and city lights and city people dazzled in the darkness.

Peering out of the windows of buses and taxis, she tried to penetrate Manhattan's mysteries. At home, she peered across the back alley, into a man's apartment. She told herself that watching him was like watching television, but she didn't tell anyone else. That man was Manhattan—close enough to touch; too far to reach.

The men she could reach were the ones she worked with, played with, slept with. The men who drove her to country inns in their foreign cars, while she sat next to them, restless and distracted. And hungry. She was always hungry in the country, always looking for something that would keep her from wanting to open the door at sixty miles an hour. The signs would fly by. SWEET CORN. FRESH-PRESSED CIDER. JUST-PICKED APPLES. HOME-BAKED PIES. But she wouldn't ask the man to stop the car until she saw the magic words: HOMEMADE FUDGE.

Her desire for chocolate had not loosened its grip on her, and she had not loosened her grip on her desire. She still looked longingly at Hershey bars every time she bought a newspaper, and still managed to pass them by every time. At the dawn of her adulthood, in the dusk of the twentieth century, in the city that doesn't sleep, the only thing she had to fear was fat.

Homemade fudge was an exception to all her rules. It might lead to something that had been lost and might not be found again. But the fudge was always too sweet, or too grainy, or not grainy enough. There was plenty of it, and plenty of men, and neither was ever enough. There was also plenty of time. Someday her prince would come; in the meantime, she would look for fudge.

She found it on Christopher Street, in a seventy-year-old shop with a sweet name. Li-Lac.

"I'll have a piece of fudge, please."

"What kind?"

"Chocolate." She liked her fudge plain too. Not plain. Pure. "This is fudge."

"You asked for fudge."

"I always ask for it. I never get it. Could I have the recipe?" she pleaded, knowing that she couldn't.

The recipe was as old as the shop; chocolate, butter, cream, and sugar, cooked in a copper pot. The rest was a secret she realized she didn't need to know. She didn't want to make fudge; she wanted someone's mother to make it for her.

From then on, she avoided Greenwich Village, and took to photographing the man across the alley with a telephoto lens. In the process, she became aware of his comings and goings; he was going out more and coming home less.

On a listless late-summer afternoon, she was in and he was out. She turned the TV on and off, opened and closed books and magazines. Nothing held her, until she came upon a mention of chocolate truffles at a shop on Madison Avenue. She tore the page out of the magazine and hailed a taxi.

Truffles, she discovered, were pieces of fudge, grown up. These truffles even looked like fudge, not round but rectangular, and except for a light dusting of cocoa powder, naked. The ingredients were nearly identical, but the name for what they became was French—*ganache*. There was also a trace of rum, which was undetectable, but would, said the man, be missed. There were no traces of sugar. Fudge was candy; a truffle was chocolate.

By the time she returned to her apartment,

the man across the alley had come home. In the time it took the sun to sink below the skyline, she devoured the contents of the entire box while waiting for him to take off his shirt. When the last light had left the room, the box was empty, and the air had turned chilly, but the man was shirtless, and Charlotte was warm, and filled.

"You can't taste the rum," said the truffle man, "but you would miss it." She missed it already.

She wanted more, and she wanted to know more. Her fascination with chocolate as subject would soon rival her desire for chocolate as object. Reading could take the place of eating, could even *justify* eating.

She learned that white chocolate was not chocolate, but cocoa butter. That milk chocolate was more milk and sugar than chocolate. She learned what she already knew: chocolate was dark.

One morning, the man across the alley was on the street, coming toward her. She could see his breath clouding the air. She could almost smell him. He was real, and so was the woman with him. The dark sweetness had become a sweet darkness.

It was the first of the forays into fantasy across back alleys and crowded rooms that enlivened a series of meaningless relationships with well-meaning men who walked through her twenties.

On her thirtieth birthday, a prince arrived. He was magical—funny, dapper, familiar. A colleague, an art director, who turned the stuff of work, and life, into adventure. He had style, and style made life look a lot better. But he was not her prince; he was someone else's.

They became friends before they became lovers. She told him about the men she didn't want, and he told her about the wife who didn't want him. At first, it was a joke, but the more they played with it, the more workable it seemed. At first, they talked and teased, and then, like overgrown teenagers, stole kisses in dark corners of studios and restaurants, sometimes even on out-of-the-way streets.

She confided in her closest friend, who had already had her own married man. It occurred to neither of them that longing would ever come before loyalty and turn them against each other. Who was to know who was The Other Woman? When the small voice whispered words like "home wrecker," she allowed her friend to remind her that good marriages could not be broken. It was true, and beside the point.

He wanted to share her life, if not her soul, and except for an edge that grew sharp with anger, she loved him more than she had ever loved anyone. When he got his divorce, she got her prince.

To the world, they had everything, and they saw themselves as they were seen, a corporate marital identity. "Young, Attractive, Talented, & Affluent. Good Morning." The things they didn't have were almost too small to notice. And for nine years, she almost didn't miss them. Dancing. Walking.

They didn't walk with their arms around each other, because they didn't fit. He was a little too tall, or she was a little too small.

When he called her Honey, she did not melt.

When they embraced, she didn't bury her nostrils in his cheek. He smelled too clean.

When they danced together, it was not like making love. When they made love, it was not like dancing.

They had everything, but the small voice said, "Not enough."

For her thirty-ninth birthday, he invited another couple to join them at The Four Seasons. "They make a great chocolate cake," he said.

"Chocolate Velvet," she replied, tasting the words. It was not a cake.

THE DARK SWEETNESS

had become A SWEET DARKNESS

It sat like a chocolate hat on the pastry cart, dark and closemouthed, until it was cut open to reveal a half-inch ribbon of yellow sponge, presumably to cut the chocolate, like a chaser. The chocolate was the rest, but it wasn't frosting or mousse or even *marquise*. The word was velvet.

It was not a cake, and The Four Seasons was not a restaurant; it was a dream about Manhattan. They had arrived at this moment together, four kids from Brooklyn, but they lived it differently.

The lives, and wives, of her husband's friends were too much alike to be interesting, with the exception of Nathan, whose life and wife were planted on one stifling suburban acre, but who seemed not to belong there himself. It was not his wild head of hair, his huge, almost black mustache, and his big, bearish body; it was something else.

Nathan looked uncomfortable and uninterested at The Four Seasons. His wife seemed hypnotized by the vast, glittering room, as high as it was wide, filled with foursomes seated around a luminous pool of water. The tables were too far apart for eavesdropping. The conversations could only be seen, but they *looked* witty. That was the point, see and be seen, eat and be eaten. Nathan's wife got the point.

As for her husband, he loved that night because he had made it happen, and because he thought he was making her happy. She had always wanted to be in that room, always wanted a bite of that chocolate hat. But the restaurant was one dream; the dessert was another. For Charlotte, chocolate was a private, if no longer secret, pleasure, and in that bright, beautiful, public place, something was lost. The room was like their marriage; it glittered, but it did not glow.

When he asked her what was wrong, she said, "Nothing. Everything is lovely," but she thought of Fleur in *The Forsyte Saga*, trying to explain the inexplicable.

"Only the moon, Michael. Only the moon."

On her husband's birthday, she gave him a set of tools, made of chocolate, and rusted with cocoa powder. The molds were authentic and beautiful, but it was the rust that drew her to them, and she carried them home, hoping they would fill the space between a wonderful man and a woman who wondered.

When he opened the box and found them, wrapped in gold linen, he smiled. When his smile faded, she could see his disappointment. He would have preferred real tools—a socket wrench, for example, calibrated metrically for his German car.

The next day, she used the toolbox as a lunchbox, in the park.

"Your teeth are beautiful." She looked up.

"You bite that—" She was charmed by his struggle for the English word.

"Hammer."

"—ferocious."

"Do you want a bite?"

She said it without thinking; she had no interest in her thoughts. He had thick hair and an accent she couldn't place, and when he took the bite, it shook her to realize how much she had missed the old familiar rush. When he kissed her in the hard high-noon light, she could taste the chocolate on his tongue, which made the distinction between his mouth and hers begin to blur. Which was what she wanted, what she had wanted for a long time, what she had feared she would never have again. She was nevertheless shocked to see herself undressing, in the mirror in his hotel room. A part of her remained aloof, judging the part that couldn't stop herself and didn't want to.

They were hungry; they swallowed each other up before eating the rest of the chocolate tools. But when she left the darkening

room, Charlotte knew that the foreigner had merely aroused her; it was the chocolate that filled her, and the empty toolbox felt like a vodka bottle in her hand.

The near-ecstasy of the afternoon gave way to the agony of a night spent lying awake beside the dear sleeping body of the man she loved. It was not just one of those things; it was one of those things that separate before from after, innocence from guilt. It did not occur to her to confess. If she never said it out loud, it would not exist outside of her mind. It would make the transition from fantasy to memory, and it would fade, faster than a photograph.

But the images did not fade, and she found herself desiring, not the stranger, but desire itself. Her guilt had destroyed her appetite for everything but chocolate, which she consumed the way guilt consumed her. Her sense of having committed a crime was so horrific that it kept her from committing another one, but it also freed her, briefly and paradoxically, to eat chocolate with abandon.

She went through all the old reliables—the truffles, the fudge, the Hershey bars—but she fixated on a jar of chocolate sauce from Wisconsin. Not only because it tasted like a melted truffle; because of the way it behaved.

It poured slowly and thickly, collecting in dark pools, coating her fingers. Its fluidity was mesmerizing; its potential to overflow, frightening. She watched her fingers disappear in the wet darkness, and appear again, until the plate was clean and her fingers were dry. She immersed a fresh red raspberry in one of the pools, and the fruit became forbidden. Eating chocolate was like having a slut for a best friend. It was a bad influence.

Finally, her husband asked the question for which he already had an answer. She looked into his worried, wounded eyes, and hesitated before shaking her head. It was true, and it was false. It wasn't an affair; it was an afternoon, long past and beside the point. For a little while, she thought she could spare both of them; she thought she could tell him the truth that mattered.

"Something is wrong." She held back her first harsh thought, hoping she could take the blame without hanging herself, and without lying. But she couldn't explain herself to herself, and he let it go.

He asked again the following Sunday, and the silent tension was broken by the sound of a ringing telephone. It was her father, asking her to join him for lunch at the Plaza, as he had done every Sunday since her mother had left him. He did not so much ask, as announce, that he would be

at their table, at the window, at noon, waiting. He always arrived before noon, having become a little fuzzy about time. Charlotte always arrived late, but she never said no. His disappointment would have been too great for either of them to bear.

When she entered the Edwardian Room, her father's face, which had softened with age, brightened as if she had brought joy with her instead of sorrow. "How lovely to see you, my dear." Something inside him had softened as well, and he took her hand and touched her cheek with real tenderness.

When they had exchanged pleasantries and news, his eyes wandered to the horses and carriages that lined the entrance to the park, and he retold the story of the uncle in the Bronx who owned the only horse and carriage in the family and once drove it all the way to Brooklyn just to give his nephews and nieces a ride.

"Do you want to ride in a horse and carriage, Daddy?"

"No," he said wistfully. He just wanted to remember.

She asked him how he was doing, and he said, "Fine. Fine," in his slightly-too-loud voice. When he asked, "And how are you, my dear?" she answered, "Okay," in her slightly-too-low voice. She didn't tell him her troubles; he didn't ask. But when they parted, he chuckled to himself as he patted her cheek with one hand, and pressed two Hershey's Kisses into her palm with the other. She wanted to cry, but instead she chuckled too, and thanked him.

The unreadable expression on her husband's face startled her when she opened the door.

"I'm not going to ask again."

The knot in her chest unraveled slightly until he added, "I know."

He was almost smiling.

The fear entered her body through her throat, and she lost the ability to swallow. "No. You don't. I am not having an affair."

"We were fine and then we weren't."

"We weren't fine. We weren't fighting, but we weren't fine."

"So now that you have me…you don't want me?"

"I've had you for nine years."

"I know…what I know."

"*What* do you know? That there was a man?" She flinched when he did. "One man? Once? That it was nothing? That it wasn't about him?" And that it wasn't worth it. She had waited a long time for that afternoon, and it lasted no longer than chocolate.

"That *I* was nothing. That it was about *me*." His sweet face turned sour, and his anger exploded into real rage. She did not try to dress his wounds, or beg his forgiveness. She wasn't leaving him; he was leaving her. Well, he was leaving her no choice.

She didn't want one. She had pushed him away because she was afraid to make a decision, or a move. Deep down in her darkness, she knew she was a coward, and she hated her fear as much as she feared her darkness.

After all the years, all the love, all the doubt, all the *furniture*, it was over with a suddenness that stunned her. She was free, but with freedom came a sadness that was paralyzing, and an emptiness that was terrifying. It could not be filled with work or friends or chocolate. She had lost all her appetites; she was stripped of her body as if it were clothing, and she no longer knew why, or even *if*, she was a photographer. She was facing forty, and she was afraid—of not having a child, a man, a job, a home.

But she left her home and her studio as well as her husband. She left the city that had become hers. She left her life. She packed a suitcase with black sweaters, blue jeans, a Leica because it was small, and a Minox because it was smaller, and flew to a place that had lived in her dreams forever.

II.

OBSESSION

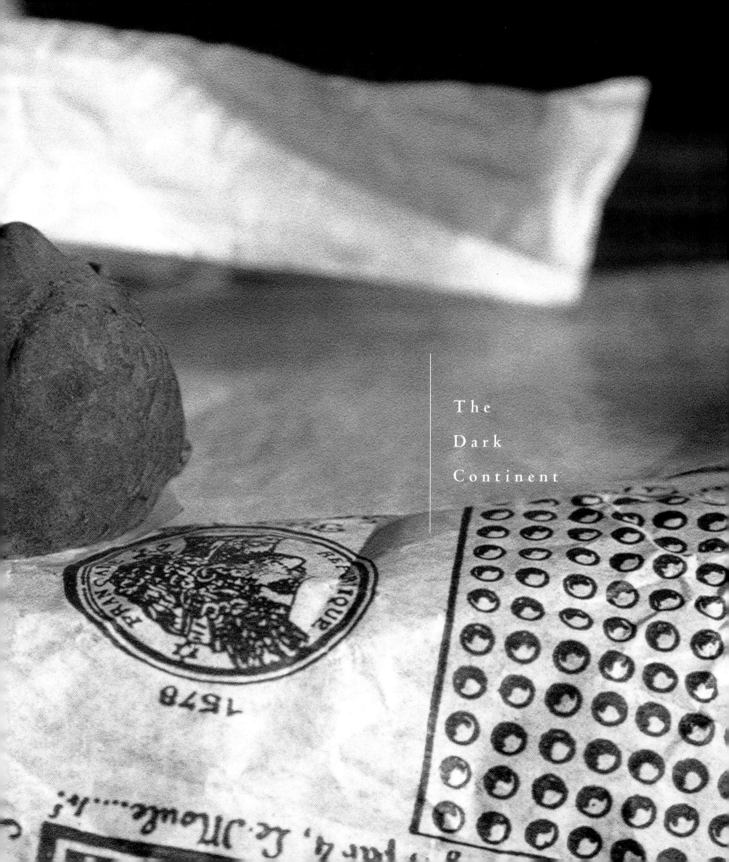

The
Dark
Continent

VIENNA

Chapter 3

The first time she walked the eighteenth-century streets in the shadow of St. Stephen's, she knew she had come home.

That was not to say that Freud's city was what she had dreamed—the Vienna of early-modern art, and angst. It was the nineteenth century, not the eighteenth, or the twentieth, that made its first impressions, and neither the scale nor the style of the Ringstrasse kept the promise of a waltz.

Vienna was a city of promise unkept, a city longing for all that was lost—the Empire, the avant-garde, the genius, the Jews. When she ventured behind the cathedral onto the exquisite little streets, her sadness and her longing were met, and matched. Even in sunlight, in summer, sorrow was intrinsic to the beauty of streets with names like Blutgasse and Judengasse. It was written in the stone.

Some of the streets were so narrow, there were only slivers of sidewalk, or none, so she walked on the flat Belgian blocks that were laid like bricks, close to the grey, cream, and ochre houses, reading the messages of other times and lives until the sounds of a strange language in the mouths of strangers had begun to sound familiar.

Gradually, her solitude was invaded by friends of friends. Being The American not only made her interesting to others,

it made them interesting to *each* other, all of them intelligent, attractive, and somehow thwarted.

She met the German at Café Landtmann. The next day he was gone with much of the rest of Vienna for the summer, having made no conscious impression. Vienna had already wrapped her in its seductive embrace, but people were still shadowy. She herself was shadowy, caught in a sort of extended out-of-body experience—insubstantial and vague, within and without.

When she began to return to her senses, it was her eyes that opened first. After a showing of *The Third Man*, she emerged from the darkness of 1949 into the color-saturated afternoon, disappointed. Like Plato's cave dweller, she found sunlit reality harsh and dull after the thrill of shadowplay on a stone wall. She wanted to see Vienna in black-and-white, balanced precariously between shadow and light.

She crossed the Ring to the Opera House and tried to imagine it in ruins. She went on to the Sacher, half-expecting Joseph Cotten to ask the concierge where he could find Harry Lime. She was longing for something that seemed to have taken place only fifteen minutes ago. Where was it? Why wasn't zither music accompanying her everywhere she walked? Where does everything go that once was? Childhood?

She could taste not only this torte, but the first one, improvised by Franz Sacher, a sixteen-year-old kitchen boy in the household of Prince Metternich. She could almost taste the very first chocolate cake, made soon after Charles VI, a/k/a Holy Roman Emperor, moved his court, and his chocolate, from Madrid to Vienna.

But there was no link to the chocolate that was drunk, sugared and spiced in Spain, and bitter and spiced in Mexico. Bitter or sweet, the Viennese no longer drank chocolate; they drank coffee, and ate pastry, not as dessert, but as itself.

The idea was brilliant—cake as the focal point of an hour, a reason to enter a *Kaffeehaus*, and be alone, but not lonely. The Viennese gave each other what they wanted—privacy and company.

"You like chocolate." She looked up. It was the German, back from the country, taller, handsomer, and darker than she remembered. He sat down, blocking the sun and invading her privacy, as if he knew he was the one who could.

"I love chocolate."

"Do you know the story of the Sacher torte?"

"Metternich?"

"He was tired of rich, creamy tortes,

Broken marriages? Does it all assume the quality of dreams and films?

Everything that would soon be foggy and insubstantial was now clear and bright. Now the water sparkled in a glass next to a perfect slice of Sacher torte, nestled against articulated waves of whipped cream. But soon the glass would be empty, and nothing but crumbs and streaks would be left on the plate.

Now the dark glaze was thick and smooth; the apricot jam was tart-sweet and laden with fruit. The cake itself was a little dry, but it was still made by hand and served *mit Schlag*, and it brought her closer to the past than architecture or art, or even music. She could ingest it.

favored by rich, creamy ladies. He request-
ed something…restrained."

"This is restraint?"

"It may be apocryphal." He shrugged, and
in the curtain of silence that surrounded
them, reached across the table for her fork,
and a bite of her torte, without taking his
eyes from hers. Suddenly, the cake in her
mouth was not dry; it was masculine. In
that moment, she knew that he wanted
her, and in the next, that she wanted him.

"I will feed you chocolate," he said.

She looked at him, and then away, and
when she looked back, he held her with
his eyes, and she couldn't look away again.
She didn't say that she could feed herself,
but he went on as if she had. "It isn't as
easy as you would think; Vienna is not
really a chocolate city. It's all pastry, and
it's not chocolate pastry that Vienna does
best. It's the *Strudel* and *Knödel*. *Äpfel*, *Topfen*,
Zwetschken, *Marillen*."

"I want chocolate."

"I know," he said, taking both of her
hands, and, holding them against the cold
white surface of the table, with only a
breath between sentences, added, "I want
to be the flame in your sadness."

It was the sort of thing she had always
wanted to hear, the thing she would have
wanted her husband to say. The fact that
less than a year later, this man would not
remember having said it was unimaginable
now. She started to tell him that she was
no longer sad, as if they had spoken about
it, but he wasn't talking about her separation. In that moment they had come home
together, to Vienna, in the time of Sacher
and Metternich, and the time before that,
and after this. When he asked if she had
been to Demel, she was so far from the
present that she nodded at first, then
caught herself and shook her head.

"I thought it was for tourists."

"It is." She laughed for the first time in
months. He made her laugh. "They have
a couple of very good cakes. You have to
know what to look for, as well as where to
look." He stood up and seemed even taller.
"Tomorrow at three."

"*Morgen um drei*," she agreed, in her best
German for travelers. She did not feel fool-
ish speaking his language badly when he
spoke hers so well. For an instant, German
felt like a mother tongue in her mouth.
And then she wondered why he wanted to
meet in the middle of the city, in the middle
of the afternoon, but by the time she left
the Sacher, she was filled with the pleasure
of longing for tomorrow. Today it was
enough to know that even the darkest
chocolate melts at body temperature.

Tomorrow would not last any longer than yesterday. Only Vienna's haunted streets would remain, and come to look more and more like the haunted German who lived there.

When she arrived at Demel at exactly three, he was there, scrutinizing twenty ravishing cakes on silver stands. She was about to face the anguish of choice, when she realized that he had chosen.

"Einmal Trüffel Torte. Einmal Dorry Torte."

Trüffel was the opposite of Sacher, voluptuous and graceful, not creamy, but rich. Dorry was creamy *and* rich, but not pretty. The forks darted across the small brown marble table in the back corner; one torte, then the other; one mouth, then the other. "I wanted to take you home with me yesterday..." He hesitated; she waited for the "but."

"...but..."

"Take me home today."

"I can't." Suddenly she knew there was another woman and the moist cake went dry in her mouth. "There *was* another woman."

"In Vienna?"

"Munich. I came to Vienna to get away from her."

Did you? she wondered, but didn't ask.

They designed a kind of courtship, a chaste but sensuous dance. Vienna was a city made for courting—contained, seductive, comfortable.

The Viennese are dreaming strollers.
When they walk, they dream.
—Otto Friedländer

It was written on a wall to illuminate an exhibition of photographs of Habsburg Vienna. When they tired of walking and dreaming, there was always sitting and dreaming, which they, and the Viennese, did just as well. Because he worked odd hours, in the theater, they would meet every day at three, or four, and again, late in the evening.

He took her to see the Brueghels at the Kunsthistorisches Museum, and to eat Gerstner torte at the museum's café. He took her to the Musikverein for Mahler and Mozart, and to Sluka for petits fours, and although, or perhaps *because*, he did not make love to her, parts of him—forearms, ears, voice—had become as delicious and potent as the cakes.

He promised to take her to his house on Irrsee in the summer, and to Bad Ischl for Zauner *Stollen*, but in the meantime he helped her find a coat for a winter she hadn't anticipated. On cold nights, they walked her streets, which were also his,

I want to be the flame

in your

SADNESS

and warmed themselves in one of the smoke-filled rooms that were to the evenings what Demel and Sacher were to the afternoons. He even took her to the theater and whispered translations in her ear. They stayed up too late in the small town Vienna became at Kalb or Kleine Café. In the corners of cafés, fingers could be nibbled like pastry. The City of Dreams had seduced them both; it was easy.

On those nights, she would lie awake, alone in a cold bed a few streets away, and relive every word and gesture until the bed was warm. She would chew them over in her thoughts until she could swallow them. The joy of wanting something within her reach calmed her, and she was sure that the joy to come when she did reach him would be worth the waiting. He would not melt in her mouth like chocolate; he would last.

She was wrong.

He didn't melt at all. He was an iceberg, he said, frozen to his rotten German soul. She heard herself tell him his soul was good and beautiful, but she couldn't hear the voice saying it was desperation that drove her, not love. "Is it her?" she asked. He said no, but she hated her anyway.

He became opaque and morose, and just when she thought he was gone for good, he gave her a book to read, the story of a bright little boy and his seductive, destructive, devouring mother. She thought he was trying to tell her something about himself that he couldn't say. He was. He was also trying to tell her something about *her*self.

When she tried to hold him to his own words, he denied them, but she heard them like a mantra.

"I want to be the flame in your sadness."

She had long left her pension, depending on the kindness and absence of friends with flats, but it was summer again, and not only was he leaving her, he was leaving Vienna. He had described his stone house so often, she felt as if she had been there, and not being there was unbearable. He offered her his flat, because it was all he had to give. Within a week, she was photographing herself, half-dressed, in his mirrors, and writing self-indulgent poetry on his paper.

"Yes," she wrote. "I smelled your shirts." And tasted Zauner *Stollen*, but not in Bad Ischl. She found it in a shop two streets away, a fat round roll of a cake—crushed hazelnuts, broken ice-cream biscuits, and not enough chocolate. It was the taste of someone else's summer.

Their lovemaking had been as disappointing to her as it was to him, but it wasn't the sex she wanted. It was the *promise* of the sex. Without it, Vienna had lost not only its beauty, but its meaning. His absence had an effect on the entire city, equal to his presence. He had not left Vienna; he had taken it with him.

One night, she let the warm light of Kleine Café lure her inside. She heard the kisses, the whispers, the promises. She left in tears to walk the stony street, pressed against the street wall as though it were winter, but the street did not embrace her either. She was a Jew in Vienna, no longer wanted.

"You said things," she whispered back to the man who promised her love and gave her chocolate.

She left Vienna with the sadness she had brought, and far more longing, and Vienna left *her*, with a taste more bitter than sweet.

MUNICH

Chapter 4

In Massachusetts, in 1692, mothers and grandmothers were executed for casting spells on adolescent girls. In Mexico, in the same century, highborn Spanish ladies were brought to trial for drinking the devil's dark blood in church. In Munich, three hundred years later . . .

Karin was a Norwegian who lived and painted in the rambling cellar of a huge house. She looked like an angel; not a tall Nordic blonde, but a gamine with a small, pale face, short, dark hair, and a voice to match.

As for Munich, it was beloved by many, including Americans who preferred it to Paris, but after Vienna it felt cold. The streets were too wide.

If Vienna was darkly feminine, Munich was darkly masculine, except in Karin's kitchen. The artists who gathered in the roughly plastered room were all female, including a neurotic Italian dog. The kitchen was enormous, but there was no bathroom, only a large tin sink for bathing, and a W.C., literally a closet. The bedroom door, directly opposite the kitchen, was always slightly ajar. All the other rooms were always a little cold, but the kitchen was warmed by the stove and the women who occupied the odd chairs surrounding the wooden table, smoking cigarettes, vilifying German and American

men, drinking chamomile tea, and eating good German bread and butter. As the darkness of the days closed in, the under-lit room grew yellow and even warmer.

One day, Karin lowered her already soft but compelling voice. "I ate a chocolate cake last night and fell madly in love." They looked up. "It appeared, after dinner, in a small apartment, a few streets from here, but it came from Bucharest. We made immediate contact." They leaned forward. "It was all chocolate — half cream, half cake. I ate it with my eyes at first, and then my mouth, and eventually my whole body; I felt lifted, and also released — a sense of absolute freedom."

She opened a drawer as though it contained a secret, took out a piece of paper, and read aloud. Her lightly accented, measured cadence became the broken English of another woman from another country, which became an incantation. Four women, artists, witches, came to the cauldron.

Charlotte was not a cook, but these were ingredients she understood, movements she remembered. Stir. Beat. Fold. She had stopped writing recipes down, because she knew she would never follow them, but she followed this one, all the way down the dizzying rivers of yellow, white, and brown, meeting, mixing, and disappearing in the bowl, promising to take her with them.

"Beat the whites of the eggs until they are stiff, and fold them, carefully, gently, into the mixture. Treat them the way you would a lover."

They carried out Karin's commands silently. Sounds were heightened—the striking of a match, the scraping of a bowl, Karin's hypnotic voice.

They made the dark cream while they waited, some more patiently than others, for the dark batter to bake and cool. "The problem is to beat in the butter a little at a time, or else you will be beating like a dog swimming."

The size of the slab of butter amazed Charlotte; she could hear her mother's voice under Karin's: "Not too much butter." This cake would be too much, and no one could stop them. There were no mothers, no men, no electric mixer. The metamorphosis of color, texture, and volume would take place under the power of their own arms.

Where there had been butter, sugar, cocoa, lemon, water, and eggs, there was now something complex, transcendent, wonderful. They stared hungrily as Karin spread the cream with a silver knife, and used another knife to cut the cake in uneven, imperfect slices. Charlotte ate hers, one near-transparent sliver at a time, oblivious to the other women, until, in her peripheral vision, she saw Sabina do the same.

Sabina was not Karin. She had dark hair, but she wore it long and wild. She wore black, but was not elfin. Her face was foreign, German, but oddly familiar. She was licking her own wounds. There was a man...

Charlotte marveled at the sameness, and the otherness; she tried to imagine what it was to *be* Sabina, and tried not to use the image to measure herself. Tried not to feel like less, because her breasts were smaller, or more, because her skin was smoother. Tried, unsuccessfully, to feel comfortable in her own skin.

She was about to turn away, not wanting to be seen watching, when Sabina lifted her gaze, and acknowledged her.

Charlotte turned back and continued the ritual, eyes on the knife as she lowered it, on the fork as she raised it. When the fork entered her mouth, she attached herself to it like a feeding infant, looking down and away in an effort to be alone with herself. When the fork was clean, she traced what was left on the plate with her fingers until it was almost as clean as the fork. She was still aware of Sabina, whose mouth softened every time she opened it to take a bite, and whose eyes narrowed, almost to the point of closing, as the cake and the cream melted together on her tongue.

Karin ate quickly, hungrily, like her dog, whose tongue shot out to lick the last bits of chocolate from the plate. Vivien's mouth moved very little, her eyes not at all. Vivien simply ate the cake, and there was no way of knowing what she felt about it. In Karin's kitchen, Charlotte learned that there were women who were like her, and women who were not.

Sabina, who must have observed her, as closely as she had observed Sabina, embraced her as they cleared the table. Before she could catch herself, Charlotte felt the strange, familiar roundness of a woman's body. She was used to embracing women in greeting, but those gestures were purposeful, predictable, containable. They were manners; they made it possible to touch another woman without feeling her, and to break away the moment before discomfort set in. Sabina's gesture was unscripted. Unsafe.

Another woman was the same, but different. The same *and* different. It was why women loved other women, and why they hated them. Sabina could be me, she thought, unless she has a man I want, and until she wants mine. The next thought arrived with a terrifying suddenness. What if Sabina were The Other Woman?

There are facts about women, and chocolate, and there are theories. The fact is, choco-late is the food most craved by women, mostly before menopause, and most acutely before menstruation. Theoretically, the craving is physical.

Theory: There is a correlation between the precipitate dip of magnesium in a premenstrual woman's body and the very high magnesium levels in chocolate. Theory: Chocolate sedates and stimulates in equal measure because it contains nearly equal amounts of sugar, which releases serotonin, and fat, which releases endorphins. Theory: Chocolate produces a lover's state of euphoria, because it contains high levels of phenylethylamine, not to mention theobromine, which behaves a little like caffeine, a little caffeine itself, traces of anandamide, which behaves like marijuana, and four hundred other compounds.

Chocolate is the most complex of foods; it contains more than twice as many substances, many of them unknown, as any other food. But there are things about chocolate, and women, that science knows even less about.

A woman reaches the peak of her sexual life at thirty-five; a man at eighteen. The fact is, women in their thirties eat more chocolate than anyone else, except adolescent boys.

The truth is, women crave chocolate when they fall in love with longing.

ZURICH

Chapter 5

She wanted to trade places with the tiny girl who was eating her candy bar as if it were a truffle, laughing as she rode round and round on the carousel in the square. The girl didn't know that chocolate could be better than this, or that it could be bad for her.

Charlotte saw herself on a carousel, at four, riding up and down, round and round, turning five, six, nine, eleven, not laughing like the other children, not really a child anymore, and already nostalgic for childhood.

Zurich was so grown-up it had begun to grow old, but it had a child's heart. Small parts of the big city remembered what it felt like to be free, but not neutral. Innocent, but not bloodless. Small, bright-colored pocket squares in the banker's grey suit.

One was a chocolate shop as big and bright as Tiffany's, some of its truffles as precious as stones. It took her a few minutes to understand that there were *truffes* and *truffes du jour*, which looked exactly alike – dark drizzled spheres filled with pure *ganache*. No liquor; no nuts. But they were not the same; *truffes du jour* were made fresh every twenty-four hours.

Charlotte bought one half-kilo for Liz, and one for herself, and ate her way to the station.

"Of course I never permit myself to eat chocolate," said the psychotherapist with the specialty in eating disorders, as she received the gift. Charlotte wanted to take the truffles out of her hands, and send them to Sabina.

There were women who were like her, and women who were not. Women who were content, or contained, and women who struggled daily against containment, willing to leave their lives and livelihoods to get to the bottom of their souls. No. She wanted to take the truffles out of her friend's hands, and put them into Sabina's mouth. She wanted to feed Sabina. The thought was an uninvited guest at an unseemly hour. Whose thought? Whose mouth? It was irrelevant. Sprungli wouldn't send the truffles to Munich, not even after she offered to pay for overnight delivery.

"Why not?"

"*Truffes du jour* cannot be shipped."

"Why not?"

"They are too fragile."

"*Why?*" she asked.

"The cream is uncooked."

"Uncooked?" she repeated, uncomprehending.

"I don't know the word in English. Ah, *ja*. Raaaoouuw."

It made them vulnerable, and poignant. At the end of the day, they lost their magic. At the end of the day, they were thrown away, like Cinderella's dress and coach and footmen. At midnight, what was once splendid and rare would become ordinary and disposable. The prince had come and gone, and at the end of the day, Liz's words resonated joylessly in her ears.

"Of course I never permit myself to eat chocolate."

Why *not*?

At the end of the day, she realized that she had not come to Zurich to see Liz; she had come in search of chocolate, and would go to Brussels, and, of course, Paris, in search of chocolate. She would eat as much of it as she wanted, until she had assimilated its power and answered its questions. Was chocolate bad for the little laughing girl? Bad for her body? Or her soul?

"Heavy, but gorgeous," said the heavy but gorgeous woman who wrapped her *pavés glacés*. Naked and cocoa-powdered, like her first truffles, but cubed and small like the paving stones they were named for.

"How heavy?" the small voice asked Charlotte. How much butter and cream had she consumed in the past weeks and months, not to mention chocolate, which contains its own butter? Cocoa butter is fat — *saturated* fat — but it has no effect on blood cholesterol level. Was chocolate bad for the little laughing girl, or was it the good Swiss butter and cream?

She took the truffles to a woman who had lived in Zurich all her long life and had never tasted them. Charlotte confided to a near-stranger that her heart had been broken in Vienna and she had taken to eating chocolates. To which the gentlewoman replied, "Oh yes," and began to speak of her husband, who was both distinguished and dashing until the day he died.

"Do you know the tale of *pavés glacés*?" she asked Frau Kupferblum.

"I knew it once." She took a decorous bite and said, "Oh yes," again, as if the truffle itself had reminded her. "Once upon a time …" she began, but hesitated, "the children of the city on the lake had forgotten how to play." She hesitated again, and took another bite. "Because they were forced to work all day long, placing small square stones in straight rows on crooked streets. But two Faeries took pity on the children. One Faerie turned the paving stones into chocolate. The other blew cocoa-powder kisses all over the little cubes until they were covered with a dusty glaze and …" The gentle voice trailed off as she put the rest of the morsel into her mouth. Her face lit up and she went on.

at the end of the day,

they were thrown away like

CINDERELLA'S DRESS...

"The Faeries gave the *pavés glacés* to the children, who remembered how to play as soon as they ate them, and never forgot for as long as they were children."

Once upon another time, there were three women in the city on the lake. Liz, who had forgotten how to ride the wooden horses over the cocoa-powdered paving stones. Charlotte, who was trying to remember. And Frau Kupferblum, who put two tiny but whole truffles in her mouth in the middle of the morning, lowered her eyes, and licked her fingers.

BRUSSELS

Chapter 6

The carpet was thin, and the furniture old. Not antique; old. But the room was large, almost grand, and there were wardrobes, iron balconies, and gauzy curtains. It was a stage on which to play the role Charlotte had written for herself a *fin-de-siècle* fantasy so beautifully seedy it would be hard to tell which century was coming to a close.

She made no effort to see the dull city beyond the splendor of the Grand Place. With a map in her hand and a list in her pocket, having plotted the shortest distances between chocolate shops, she walked purposefully from one to the other, bought a few chocolates in each, and waited until she was out of sight of the proprietor to taste them. Rarely did she go back for more.

She dispensed with the famous names ruthlessly. Godiva. No. Neuhaus. Leonidas. No. No. Finally, she opened a door that said, simply, MARY, and entered a time warp. She was confused at first. The chocolates were not immediately visible in the glass cases, and she was asked, in a tone that implied that she had stumbled into Cartier by mistake, if she was looking for a gift.

"Oui, Madame."

It was not really a lie. She knew no one in Brussels; no one knew her. She couldn't hear the voice accusing her of overindulgence and self-absorption. She could give herself gifts. She was permitted to eat nothing but chocolate. To speak to no one except to say *"Bonjour, Madame. Merci, Madame. Au revoir, Madame."* To learn that the dark secret of Belgian chocolate, neither dark nor chocolate, was *crème fraîche.*

She returned to the faded luxury and fading light of her boudoir with three stiffly wrapped boxes. She undressed, and unwrapped the boxes as if she had received them from a man, from *three* men, trying to choose among them. Vanilla-bean-flecked *crème fraîche* from Mary. Or coffee *crème fraîche* from Wittamer. Or *crème fraîche* and caramel from Manon. She couldn't choose, so she kept eating until she had eaten too much.

It was all too much—the enormous bed, the silk lace lingerie, the oversize gilded mirror, the bare legs draped over the fat wooden arm of a velvet chair, the open, beribboned boxes. She had set the scene perfectly, but she had forgotten to write the script and hire the actors. It was a one-woman show—theatrical, but undramatic.

She looked at what remained in the boxes—picked-over and melting—and felt uncomfortably full. She turned on the overhead light and saw herself in the mirror— a nearly naked forty-year-old woman,

streaked with chocolate. She laughed so she wouldn't cry.

It was well after midnight. The footmen had turned back into mice, but the prince had not come. It was too much, but it still wasn't enough. In a moment of near-panic, she reached for the telephone.

Months before she left her husband, he had had a falling-out with Nathan, an event even less expected than the separation. Nearly two years later, she called her soon-to-be-ex-husband's ex-friend's office, from a hotel room in Brussels in the middle of the night. He was less surprised than she was. She told him about Vienna, and New York. She told him everything, and he still wasn't surprised. It took ten minutes to remake a connection she didn't know they'd had.

"What are you doing in Brussels?"

"I was taking pictures in Vienna."

"What are you doing in Brussels?"

"Eating chocolate."

"Why?"

"I've always wanted to."

"Was it what you always wanted?"

"Yes, but—"

He stopped her. "I think you should come home."

"After Paris."

"How long have you been in Europe?"

"A year...or so."

"Come home."

"I will."

She waited until dawn to call London.

The sun was up; he should be. "Bob?" A grunt. "Hi."

"Mmmm."

"It's me."

"Who?" he mumbled.

"Charlotte."

"Where?"

"Brussels."

"Why?"

"They have good chocolate."

"We have better." He was waking up.

"Since when?"

"Since . . . When were you here last? When are you coming?"

"I'm just calling. I'm on my way to Paris."

"London is on your way to Paris."

"It's a detour."

"I'll buy you chocolate."

"Bob. I'm in Brussels. I've been to Zurich. The next stop is Paris."

"Have you never heard of the chocolate houses of Mayfair?"

"In what century?"

"The seventeenth."

"I think it's over."

"Also the eighteenth. Trust me."

"Not about chocolate."

LONDON

Chapter 7

"By the turn of the eighteenth century there were chocolate houses all over London," droned Bob as he led her from Maida Vale to Chelsea, on foot. "The men would begin to arrive at four-thirty in the afternoon and spend the evening playing cards and talking politics."

"The men?" She had awakened in London, wishing it were Paris, where women were not only welcome, but worshiped. She followed Bob for what felt like miles, a Japanese wife with a camera around her neck. "Is this about getting it wholesale?"

He shook his head. "Fresh." He had an educated, demanding palate, at least as obsessive as hers. It was why she had come. He knew where to go, or he would find out.

Her passion for chocolate drove her down the same yellow-brick road as her passion for passion; she was seeking the elusive, illusory ideal, always hoping, and fearing, that she would find it.

Finally, they found the sliver of a shop in the King's Road. "We'll have a pound of house truffles, and a Manjari bar," he said, without consulting her.

"Is that the English equivalent of a Hershey bar?"

"Hardly. It's the English version of an eat-ing chocolate made from the finest French *couverture . . . couverture*, supposedly meaning chocolate used as an outer covering, but, more often, meaning chocolate with a high percentage of cocoa. In this case, sixty-four," he added before she could ask.

Whatever it was, it was perfectly balanced between bitter and sweet. "God, this is good."

"This is the curtain raiser. Taste the truffles."

"Who makes them?"

"Jo."

"*J-o?*"

He nodded.

"A woman."

"A woman."

These were not ladylike Swiss truffles, or hard-edged New York truffles; they were round, but a little rough, and uneven, like many different but beautiful breasts. They looked as though they had grown wild somewhere in France, but they were made in England, of Manjari, and single and double English cream, and a bit of French butter.

"Also Caraibe," Bob added. "Sixty-six percent. Another *grand cru*. There are three; the best of the best. It has to do with the

her passion for chocolate drove
her down the same yellow-brick
road as her passion for

passion

beans—these are single bean varieties—as well as the process. Valrhona grinds to a fineness of thirteen microns; they conche for four days."

"Why do you know that?"

"Why don't *you*?"

"Who is Jo?"

"A therapist . . . in training." Another witch.

"She says it's actually therapeutic, using her hands, and her senses, all six of them," offered the serious young woman behind the counter.

"She doesn't use a thermometer," added Bob. Charlotte looked at him, looking at her. He was not unattractive. On the contrary, he was handsome and heterosexual. As they say in England, he had all the qualities, or most of them. He too wanted to feed her chocolate, but unlike the German, he knew only how to buy it. He was a lawyer; he didn't miss anything, not a film, not a trick, not a comma, but something was missing in him. Something not visible, not palpable. She couldn't feel him, not with all six of her senses.

"Can I drop you somewhere on my way to the office?"

"I'll walk."

"I'll book the Ivy for dinner after the theater.

The curtain comes down at ten-fifteen."

"Okay."

"Okay."

She walked as far as the nearest bench and opened the little sack. Bob had already eaten his share; eating was almost an afterthought for him. He ate chocolate like Vivien. Not like Sabina.

Charlotte closed her eyes until she could see Sabina, fingers and mouth in thrall to her sliver of Romanian cake. This time, Charlotte opened the half-open door to Karin's bedroom. She wasn't thinking; it wasn't happening. This time, she followed Sabina into the half-light. When Sabina put her arms around her and hugged her to her breasts, she felt them as breasts. When Sabina lay down on Karin's bed, and looked up at her, she lay down next to her. When she felt Sabina's breasts in her hands, she felt Sabina's hands on her breasts. When Sabina turned her face to hers, she did not look away. When Sabina opened her mouth, she opened hers. When Sabina moved the inch between them, she could feel the thickness of her own tongue against her bottom teeth, and Sabina's mouth against hers. The same, and different; different and the same. But she couldn't kiss Sabina, not even in a dream.

The sound of a sweet and pungent voice

opened her eyes. A young man with a guitar was singing for his supper. She hid behind her camera, like a child who thinks she can't be seen if she closes her eyes. She watched his face change, from almost ugly to almost handsome. He had a scar and a birthmark and bits of a beard, the same noncolor as his hair. He was built to fight in the street, muscular and scrappy, but slender. There was something oddly poetic and touching, almost tragic, about him. He was a wide-eyed boy and a beaten man—hopeful, but used up.

"Are you a photographer?" he asked between songs.

"Are you a singer?"

He laughed, and she offered him a truffle, which he accepted gratefully, and ate like Karin's crazy dog. One truffle would lead to another. Hours later, she let the question in her mind out of her mouth. "How old are you?"

"Twenty-two."

"God."

"How old are *you*?"

"I thought you were thirty."

"I thought you were twenty-nine."

"*Thirty*-nine."

"You're beautiful."

"Forty. I'm forty."

She was almost old enough to be his mother, who was, she was later to learn, all of forty-two, but he seemed older, and not only because he was world-weary. They spent the afternoon at play, until it was time to go home for supper.

"Stay in London," he pleaded.

"I can't." But as she said the words, she leaned into him and nearly swooned. The bad girl finally spoke up.

"Come to Paris."

"I can't."

"Yes. You can."

They both knew what she meant, although they made a wordless agreement not to mention it again. She would pay. She would pay all the money she had to eat chocolate in bed, with him, in Paris. She didn't tell Bob; she couldn't.

"Where are you going?"

"Paris. You knew I was going to Paris." He knew a lot of things. Bob was a man of means, integrity, and substance, but she was going to Paris with a busker, because she could smell him.

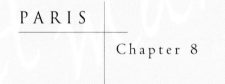

PARIS

Chapter 8

In a small hotel in the Marais, a ravishing seventeenth-century room opens onto a balcony overlooking a courtyard. In the seventeenth century, women greeted men in this room with a question.

"Voudrez-vous du chocolat?"

But they would fall in love with Paris first, using it, as lovers had always done, as an aphrodisiac, arms wrapped tightly around each other — one person with two pairs of eyes and four legs. There was no rush to see anything, so they would see everything without effort or judgment. They would see that all of Paris was beautiful and erotic. They would prolong the agony to heighten the ecstasy.

It was October, and the light was even more beautiful because it was becoming scarce. If it was possible to paint this light, she thought, it should be possible to photograph it. She had meant to photograph the light in Vienna, but she had gotten caught in the shadows. This was different; his desire surpassed hers, and her desire confounded her. When she glanced at him, quickly, from a distance, she saw a boy; at close range, he had no age and neither did she. He was like a shadow picture; in a while, the background becomes the foreground. The shadow becomes the light.

In bed, he was a man. He took the lead in the first, slow, catlike dance, pawing as she purred, licking as she stretched, biting as she scratched, until she felt as if she could be penetrated anywhere. When he did enter her, he said, "Don't move," and they stayed together, glued together, without speaking, for what could have been an hour, or a minute. He told her that he loved her and she was so moved she said it back.

Paris was the last stop. Mecca, Jerusalem, Oz. But even the *chocolatiers* of Paris could not compete with him, and for three days, she left her list behind. For three days, they wandered the streets in a languid haze, never venturing so far from their bed that they couldn't reach it on foot in ten minutes.

On the fourth day they stumbled into Angelina, a *salon de thé* in which well-dressed, well-mannered Parisian women found themselves in the afternoons. When he followed her to the center of the large, crowded room, she could feel them watching; she could feel herself shining in the light of their eyes. When she was seated, she returned the glance of the woman at the next table, and when the woman, who had Sabina's eyes, averted them, a bowl of whipped cream and a little Limoges pitcher streaked with something darker and thicker than tea came into focus. It wasn't coffee either. It was chocolate.

She looked around. There were Limoges pitchers on all the little tables, and bowls of freshly whipped cream. All the women were drinking chocolate, or pouring it, from little pitchers into big cups, ready to receive the cream. Soon they had their own Limoges pitchers, painted with green flowers and "Angelina" in cursive green letters. When they took their first simultaneous sips, their eyes locked in recognition.

"Melted truffles," he said. She had thought so too, but her voice had gotten stuck in her throat, reveling in the warmth of the unctuous liquid—so thick it could be eaten, so smooth it was impossible not to drink.

"Qu'est-ce que c'est?" she asked the brusque, matronly woman who had served them, but seemed oblivious to the powers of the objects she carried on silver trays.

"Chocolat chaud."

"Oui, mais qu'est-ce que c'est?"

"Le chocolat et le lait."

"C'est tout?"

"Et la patience," she added, somewhat derisively. Charlotte thought she said *"la passion."*

Here was the link that was missing in Vienna. A path to Charles V of Spain and Cortés and Moctezuma. Here was the Spanish princess betrothed to the French

King, arriving in Paris with a carved and gilded chocolate box and a maid, whose only task it was to beat chocolate with a *molinet* for an hour before serving it to her mistress in bed. She could see the look of desire on the face of La Molina, who was permitted only to smell her lady's chocolate.

Charlotte closed her eyes and drank from the Limoges cup. She was permitted. She was the Queen of France.

"Voudrez-vous du chocolat?" she said, before refilling his cup.

He drank it almost in one gulp; he was a young blood in a Covent Garden chocolate house at four-thirty in the afternoon, and the drink was an elixir, a potion, an initiation. As another, wiser Englishman once said, it was the end of the beginning. That day ended at four-thirty, and the night began.

"L'addition, s'il vous plaît."

"Oui, Madame."

At five, they were in their heavy, dark bed. "Take off your underpants," he said. She did what he said. "Turn onto your stomach."

He lifted her short black skirt above her waist, and caressed the curves of her hips for a long time before he parted her legs, just enough for his fingers to intrude, and even then, he didn't touch the insides of her thighs, but only the wet hairs between them.

"Open your legs."

He asked if she wanted more, and before she could form the word with her lips, he withdrew his hand, and she could feel all of the air in the room between her legs. She was exposed; it didn't occur to her to wonder whether it was the same as being open. It didn't matter; he didn't leave her like that for long.

The next day, they went beyond their *quartier* and crossed the Seine. The streets of St. Germain no longer belonged to Picasso and Janet Flanner, but they were paved with the same beloved cobblestones, and the waiters were still arrogant at Deux Magots.

"What will become of us?" he asked.

When she smiled, and said, "We'll always have Paris," he didn't know she was quoting. He seemed not to have a past, not even a childhood. He talked about her, instead of himself. He said she saw endings in place of beginnings. He knew the answers without knowing the questions, but she couldn't help correcting his English, not to mention his French. It would be easier if he were just a kid. What do women want, Dr. Freud? To want.

The darkest chocolate is not eighty, ninety, or ninety-nine percent cocoa. It is not the one that looks darkest, and tastes bitterest; it is the one that tastes bittersweetest. The darkest chocolate is not only dark; it is smooth, fine, complex, pedigreed, and French.

"I want chocolate."

"You shall have chocolate."

"I want Manjari."

In Paris, Manjari was no farther than the nearest *pâtisserie*, and for her, it was still the perfect bittersweet balance. For him, the balance tipped at seventy percent cocoa, in Guanaja. It was the most aromatic, and perhaps the most exotic, but it was too bitter for her. That night, he took her to the other side of his sweetness. He made her wait too long.

The next day, they walked the streets as usual, but with an unusual sense of purpose. She had remembered her list, and she couldn't forget it. Constant. Chaudun. Hevin. Maison. She could hear the names in her head like a song. The names and the words of chocolate are French. *Couverture. Truffe. Bonbon.*

In France, chocolate has depth and chocolates are pure. Food is art, and chocolate is food, regarded with the respect given to cheese and wine. But chocolate does not improve with age; *ganache* ought to vanish somewhere between the tongue and the palate. Why did she want to possess what could only be consumed?

She consumed it all. Michel Chaudun's truffles. Jean-Paul Hevin's *pralines*. Christian Constant's exotic, erotic perfumes. Ylang-Ylang. Verbena. Vetiver. Charlotte never met any of these Frenchmen, but she knew them all, and they knew her.

"Let's go home." Her English boy had had enough.

"There's one more."

"No more."

"But it's—"

"On the list?"

"Yes."

"Am *I*?"

She let him lead her back to the dark bed, allowed him to use the same slow, masterful touch, but with a harder edge. Something had shifted, from the heightening of her pleasure, to the heightening of his. It was apparent in his eyes; the more heat they reflected, the colder they became.

The next morning, she looked into those eyes and asked for more chocolate.

"One more."

"Bloody hell."

"The best one."

"Why wasn't it the first one?"

"I was saving it."

When they approached the big wooden doors with brass letters on a street crowded with women and their jewelry, he stopped in his tracks.

La Maison de Chocolat. Paris. New York.

"New York?"

Yes, she had been to the shop in New York. No, it wasn't enough. This wasn't a shopping trip; it was a pilgrimage.

If Paris was Oz, Robert Linxe was the wizard. His *bonbons* were subtle, layered marriages of cocoa and fruit, cocoa and spice, cocoa and cocoa. His truffles left final, unexpected, whole notes. With six shops on two continents, he couldn't possibly make his chocolates himself, but he made every one, whether or not he ever touched them.

Charlotte was in heaven, and in control, shining, without jewelry. Her English boy, suddenly ragged, saw it; she let him see.

"Let's get out of here."

"We just got here."

"I'm stuffed."

"Four days ago you were starving."

He scowled at her before slithering out the door like the rocker he was.

"L'addition, s'il vous plaît."

"Oui, Madame."

Paris swallowed him up faster than she could get her American Express card back. When she opened the door to their empty room, she was almost relieved.

He was out on the balcony.

"I couldn't find you."

"Here I am."

"I still can't. I can't even smell you."

"I'm not chocolate."

"I'm sorry."

"Don't apologize."

"I'm s—" She caught herself, and reached out to stroke his hair, but he flinched like a moody adolescent. When she put her arms around him, he let his own arms hang at his sides, and eased back against the exterior stone wall, leaning on it, his mouth against her ear, her hands pinned against the wall.

"Can you smell me now?" he whispered. She closed her eyes and nodded, while he raised his hands to lift her skirt and lower her silk underpants to the tops of her thighs. It was late morning; they were in full view of the windows on the courtyard. Over and over, he asked her if she could smell him while he leaned back so she would have to lean forward. He held her skirt above her waist with one hand, and played with the widening space between her legs with the other. Over and over, she nodded, like one of those dolls in the back of a car. She was either oblivious, or keenly aware, that the lower half of her body was exposed. She pressed herself against him, but he did not melt into her, and she tried not to kiss him or cry.

"Please," she said, finally, in desperation.

As soon as the word was out, he took his hand away, leaning forward against her until they were both vertical. Before she had a chance to steady herself, he left her there and went inside. She heard the door of the room open and close. Still breathless, she went cold. She pulled up her underpants, pulled down her skirt, and ran down the stairs after him to prowl the streets they had wandered, and to return, hours later, to find a message from Nathan, and four parcels from four regions of France at the desk. She opened them as she made her way nervously up the stairs.

The first was from Henri Le Roux. It was filled with truffles made with truffles. Real ones. *Truffes de truffe.* The second, from Joel Durand, who numbered his chocolates, and had sent numbers 1, 3, 13, 14, and 16. The third, from André Cordel; and the fourth, from Michel Belin, who had enclosed a note, with hand drawings and five words—Cinnamon, Licorice, Ginger, Jasmine, and Orgeat. *Orgeat?*

All the boxes were from Bob, of course, still trying to give her what he thought she wanted. The English boy was gone, of course, and so were his clothes.

"L'addition, s'il vous plaît."

"Oui, Madame."

On a beautiful day, the City of Light had grown darker than the City of Dreams. Charlotte surrendered, but not to Paris; she never saw Paris, not even through a lens. She succumbed to the wizards—the men who knew magic and used it in a conspiracy against her until she was spellbound and blind. With minutes and a few francs to spare, she bought a pocket French dictionary at the airport.

Orgeat (n.): A syrup of almonds and orange-flower water.

She succumbed to the wizards—the men who knew magic and used it in a conspiracy against her until she was spellbound and blind.

III.

R

REDEMPTION

The
American
Dream

WALPOLE

Chapter 9

Having eaten her way through the boxes, and across the Atlantic, Charlotte spent the rest of the longest day of her life at the wheel of a rented car, wending her way to New Hampshire.

She couldn't face New York. Not in October, at its most beautiful. Not without more chocolate.

At five minutes before closing time, she hastily opened what seemed like the wrong door. Until she saw the ten-pound blocks of raw chocolate on the metal shelves. The dipping chocolate in the vat on the wooden table. The chocolate tempering on the stove visible in the back room. It looked nothing like Paris; it looked like a kitchen.

A mercurial man in chocolate-covered whites offered her a truffle. "What does it taste like?"

"Paris."

"Valrhona," he said, as if it were a code word. She knew the code. "And freshness; *ganache* starts to deteriorate in twenty-four hours."

"I know."

"The better the chocolate, the better the chocolate. The better the butter, the cream, the ginger, the oranges, the tea, the coffee, the vanilla . . . the better the chocolate." He

talked as fast as he moved, from stove to table to sink, in long, jittery sentences. "And very thin walls. The French think with all their senses . . . you shouldn't have to bite through something to get to something else."

No, she thought, you shouldn't. And begged silently for another truffle.

"Anyone could do this . . . anyone who spent the time . . . and the money . . . nobody does . . . not here."

This was the New World, or maybe it was just New England, or New Hampshire, but here there were no officious salespeople hiding behind fancy storefronts. No glass and brass cases. "One more thing . . . important . . . the flavor of the chocolate should dominate any other flavors . . . which should always come from real food . . . not extracts . . . slightly."

And no secrets. Just a self-effacing wizard, far from Oz.

"I'll take two dozen mice to go," she said, in a gap between his sentences.

When she opened the beautifully plain wooden box, four straight rows of rodents looked up at her. She picked one up by his red silk tail, snatching him out of formation, and bit off one ear. And then the other. And then his head. Inside the body, she could see the chocolate flesh, and she could taste it, inside the severed head. Real *ganache* in a make-believe mouse.

Suddenly, she stopped savoring it and began to chew it hard, gnashing her teeth in anger. She was Cinderella, and the head belonged to one of the footmen who had turned back into mice. She was Clara and the head belonged to a mean little boy who broke her Nutcracker and was transformed into a man-size mouse. She was Charlotte, and the head in her mouth was *his*. She chewed it until she was chewing on her saliva.

She bit off another head, filled with *Schokolade*, and she devoured it, just as that man, that mouse, had feared she would. Soon all the mice had faces, and all the faces had names.

Arthur. Charlie. David. Dan. Harry. Howard. Jack. Jerry. Larry. Louis. Markus. Norman. Owen. Robin. Stefan. Tony. Zack. The boy who adored her in first grade and moved away. The boy who gave her a perfect summer but not the fall. The boy next door who fell in love with the girl across the street. The man across the alley. The men who pushed her away by holding on too tight, and the men who just pushed her away. She had kept them in reserve, like old toys she had outgrown years ago but couldn't bear to throw away.

The boys in the boybox.

One after another, she bit off their heads, chewing some of them into tiny unrecognizable pieces, swallowing others almost whole. She smelled fear and she wanted blood. She wanted the Nutcracker to slay the five-headed Mouse King and turn into a prince, but she knew he wouldn't. The story would not come true, but the story *was* true, as all fairy tales are. As all children know.

She had to slay all the mice herself.

The bed became a battlefield, strewn with broken, decapitated bodies and disembodied tails. The violence was liberating, but it left her off-balance. She felt disoriented, queasy, sick. Of chocolate or of men?

She ran outside to get air, but there was none. She ran back inside and called Nathan, who, thankfully, was still in his office. The sound of his voice in her ear was a balm, steadying her until she could tell him the whole sorry, sordid story.

"Do you want to know what I think or do you want sympathy?"

"Both."

"I think you write these plays and cast them."

"Where's the sympathy?"

"You don't need it."

"I'm miserable, Nathan."

"That's the play. You have a core of steel."

"How do you know that?"

"I saw it the first time I saw you."

"Everyone else sees sadness."

"Take pictures."

"What do you mean?"

"It's not a metaphor."

"Nathan—"

"Go away."

"I just got back. I haven't even called my mother."

"Go the other way. Go to Hawaii."

"I hate Hawaii."

"You've never been there."

"Neither have you."

"You would love the light."

"No. I wouldn't. Oh God. You called Paris. I'm sorry."

"I needed someone to talk to."

"I thought you were trying to save me."

"I was trying to save myself." She waited for the other shoe. "We're separated."

"I'm so sorry." Sorry for his pain; sorrier for not having been there to ease it. She had been too busy reveling in Nathan's knowledge of her, and relying on it, to know him back.

"Tell me." And he did. "I love you, Nathan," she said an hour later. It surprised both of them, but there was nothing romantic about it.

"Call your mother."

"Call yours."

"She's dead."

He made her laugh, but he didn't make her want him. Like Bob? Not like Bob, but not like the German, or the busker, or the foreigner either. The men she wanted were not the men who wanted her.

"Hello."

"Hello."

"Thank God."

"Hello, Mother."

"Are you in Europe?"

"No."

"New York?"

"New Hampshire."

Arthur. Charlie. David. Dan. Harry. Howard. Jack.
Jerry. Larry. Louis. Markus. Norman. Owen.
Robin. Stefan. Tony. Zack.

The boys who made her wait. The boys who made
her want. The man who promised her love
and gave her chocolate.

"I thought you were in Europe."

"I *was* in Europe."

"You didn't call."

"I'm calling."

"I have something to tell you."

"What?"

"It's not good."

"What?"

"Your father is"—a shiver of fear ran through her—"in the hospital." She waited, her heart in her throat. "Of course, it's his heart. But they don't know . . . or they don't say. You know how they are, doctors. You should have called."

She let the silence hang between them like the air in the stuffy Brooklyn apartment. Her mother still lived there, and was still legally married to her father, but she had relinquished her role as wife, and, in some bitter way, had bequeathed it to her daughter.

The thought of her father, helpless and heartsick, tore at her own battered heart, but she was incapable of getting back into the car that night. Everything was breaking down. Nothing was what it had been. She cleared the bed of silk tails and paper cups, and laid herself down to weep in the dark void. The friendly darkness, her father would say, when it frightened her.

He died before she got there. He died alone. She had finally said no. "No, Daddy. I can't meet you at the Plaza at noon. I'm busy. I'm tired. I'm sad. I'm sorry." She had disappointed him for the first and last time, and she couldn't bear it.

She spent the night at his apartment, because, she told herself, she had nowhere else to go. It was ghoulish and lonely, and she got out of her dead father's warm bed at midnight to buy a Hershey bar at the newsstand on the corner, hoping it would help, knowing it wouldn't. With a crumpled candy wrapper in her hand, she crumpled her exhausted body into a ball.

Arthur. Charlie. David. Dan. Harry. Howard. Jack. Jerry. Larry. Louis. Markus. Norman. Owen. Robin. Stefan. Tony. Zack. The boys who made her wait. The boys who made her want.

The man who promised her love and gave her chocolate.

THE BIG ISLAND

Chapter 10

High in the sulfurous air, waiting for the bubbles to break through the surface of the moonscape, she felt even queasier. Here was the equivalent of the shaky ground she had always stood on, bubbling to the surface, glistening and threatening. But it did not shoot its fire madly into the sky; it belched and hissed like a radiator in a Brooklyn apartment, and so did she.

Belched. Yawned. Shivered. Sweated. Scratched. Sneezed. Farted. Croaked. It had all happened before, but not all at once. The underground pressure had become unbearable; she felt as if she would erupt, but didn't. She was forced to face the parts of herself that were not sweet, or delicate, and would not go on swimming in a hot lake under cold ground. The only way out was in. There were no truffles in Hawaii, no silk-tailed mice, and no bad boys. Nothing to devour but her own dark heart. Demon, dybbuk, devil.

"The darkness is not friendly, Daddy."

She drove like a lunatic, all the way down the fiery mountain, and beyond, not stopping until she came to a field of amazing trees, laden with deep-purple and burnt-orange pods, as big as gourds. It was a wonderland—natural and fantastic.

"Strange fruit," she whispered to the trees, mesmerized.

"Cacao," said a voice behind her.

She turned around to find a man standing there, smiling at her astonishment. "Chocolate," he said, translating. It wasn't a language problem.

"It can't be."

"It is." He took a flat, round, quarter-size piece out of his pocket.

"Cacao doesn't grow here."

"Nothing grew here once. But I'm impressed that you know enough to get it wrong. No one in the civilized world knows anything about cacao."

For nearly five centuries, a line had divided crown from colony, oppressor from oppressed, culture from nature, chocolate from cacao, and this man had erased it. "Hawaiian Vintage Chocolate," he said, offering it to her. "Born and made in the U.S.A."

"Vintage?" She was still not used to hearing the words "Hawaiian" and "chocolate" in the same sentence.

"Chocolate is the wine of the Americas."

"I'm off the stuff."

"All you need is one." Was he pushing… or flirting?

"One drink?"

"One *pistole*." She hesitated. "Come on. It took eight years. I traveled the world in search of beans. Java for Criollo. And Venezuela. Trinidad for Trinitario. Beans that grow wild in the rain forest, and Gran di Floria, the godfather bean … one botanical step before *Theobroma cacao*." He grinned. "Food of the gods."

"Whose gods?"

"The Aztecs', but Mayans worshiped them first. Maybe even Toltecs. Cacao was a gift from Quetzalcoatl, god of knowledge and culture…especially agriculture. In Hawaii, he's Lono; in Greece, Dionysus."

"My point."

"Dionysus, not Bacchus. One glass of wine, not a bottle. A piece of chocolate, not a box."

"It isn't that simple."

"It's the most complex plant on the planet; this plant, even more so. It's a new bean, crossbred from all the others, growing in who knows how many layers of volcanic soil." He took a breath. "But it *is* a plant. Elemental. Organic."

"Organically *grown?*"

"Organically… and lovingly."

"What about pests?"

"No pests in paradise; it's too far from the mainland."

"No insects?"

"I didn't say that. Come with me."

She went. She was smitten, with him, with Hawaii, with cacao.

"After the harvest … and before the drying…" He picked a purple pod and hacked it open with a machete. Inside, it was lavender-white, almost iridescent, and sticky. Pulp. It looked less like chocolate than anything she'd ever seen.

"That's it?"

"This is it," he said, removing a bean from inside the pulp, like an embryo from a sac. "But that's part of it. Taste it."

It was juicy, and fruity; it was fruit. After a beat, and with a slightly theatrical flourish, Jim opened a large wooden box, unleashing a smell so sweet and pungent she turned away. When she turned back, embarrassed, she saw it—a steaming, insect-filled ooze, a living, breathing, horror-movie slime.

"God."

"I think so."

Charlotte laughed. He made her laugh. "What is it?"

"It's fermenting. When you make a new batch, you use a piece of wood from the old one, like yogurt … or sourdough starter. The wood attracts insects, which attract a hundred and thirty-two bacteria and yeasts."

"You've counted."

"Come here."

"No."

"Touch it."

"I'm not good at this."

"It doesn't have teeth."

"Is it sanitary?"

"If it was sanitary, it wouldn't ferment. Bend your arm, and dip your elbow in it. Just a few inches. I want you to feel it." Why did he want her to feel it? What did he want her to feel? "Come on." It was hot. It was alive—the slimiest thing she had ever felt on her skin, and some slimy part of her loved it.

"This is where chocolate's flavor is formed—its roundness and depth. It's the primal, low-tech stuff. What happens in the factory … the roasting, grinding, pressing, refining, conching, tempering … all about texture."

"It doesn't come off."

"It's a souvenir." But he grabbed a wet towel from the side of the box and wiped her arm with it in a way she could only describe as ambiguous. "It's mostly cocoa butter." The skin on her arm was left clean, but slightly slippery, and as soft as the skin on her breasts. The slimy part of her wanted to bathe in that box.

She told him. He laughed. His laugh was attractive, but what made him irresistible was what he knew.

"I'll take the chocolate," she said, with a half-smile.

"Kona 'Ninety-four. Hodges Estate."

"It's a different food," she said, as it assumed the shape of her tongue.

"Voluptuous."

"Yes."

"Can you taste the flowers?"

"Yes."

"Everything is in it. The bean. The weather. The soil. The bacteria. And the past."

She was staring into the mouth of another crater, about to jump off the edge, when the sun lit on something gold. A ring. A wedding ring. How could she not have seen a wedding ring? She shifted her gaze from his hands to hers and watched the

His wife was not The Other Woman;
she was *another* woman.

SHE WAS ME.

pistole in her palm, melting in a perfect circle, caught between the warmth of her hand and the light of the sun.

All circles were perfect. Sun. Moon. Earth. Ring.

Suddenly, the question of flirting did not need to be answered. Charlotte would not do the dance with him; she would dance with Dionysus. She would eat the Godhead.

His wife was not The Other Woman; she was *another* woman. She was me.

TUILA

Chapter II

I am in Oaxaca, in the *mercado*, buying beans from a *cacaotero*. His father was a *cacaotero*, and all of his grandfathers for forty centuries. I also buy a chocolate pot, a *molinillo*, and a *jícara*.

I take my beans to a grinder who grinds them with cinnamon, almonds, and sugar, by hand, on a *metate*.

I stir madly with the *molinillo* to produce a froth, as if my worth depended on it, which, in view of the look on the face of the man watching me, it does. I hold the pot high in my left hand, the *jícara* low at my right hip, pouring back and forth until the liquid forms a head. I offer it to him; he takes it.

I look down, but the *jícara* is not empty; it is filled with *xocolatl* thick enough to eat, redolent of chilies and vanilla, and it is made of gold. It is for soldiers, priests, and rulers, who drink from it before battles, rituals, ravagings. I kneel at the feet of my ruler, Moctezuma. I am his wife, among all of his wives. We serve him, and his guest, a white-faced god whose arrival was foretold. But Cortés is not a god; he is a conqueror who will tear *xocolatl* from its root.

I look up, but there is only one man, one God-King. We are in the forest at the center of the earth, four thousand years ago.

He offers me one of the golden goblets.

"But you are my King."

"And you are my Queen."

"Xochiquetzal," I whisper, remembering my name, closing my eyes in rapture, as we drink together.

When I opened them, United Flight 28 from Los Angeles was making its descent into Kennedy.

NEW YORK

Chapter 12

Nine hours before midnight on New Year's Eve, I went to the Plaza to meet my father. I sat on Zelda's fountain looking into the window. I saw him at our table, gazing wistfully at the horse-drawn carriages. I heard him tell the story of the uncle in the Bronx. I heard him singing me to sleep with old love songs, as if they were lullabies. But I couldn't hear us talk, because we didn't. There were stories, and songs, but no conversation. I never told him about my love life, because my lovers were his rivals. My father adored me instead of loving me. Then he left me. *He* left *me*.

I felt the old familiar tears tightening my throat. I walked away with a wet face. The phone was ringing when I entered my new apartment.

"What time tonight?"

"Ten."

"I'll be there."

"I loved the light."

"Did you take pictures?"

"Not with a camera." I hesitated. "I found chocolate."

"Only you."

"I'm not going to eat it; I'm going to drink it. What do you know about drinking chocolate?"

"Nothing."

"I'm trying to make it like Angelina, but it's not thick enough."

"Did you ask Angelina?"

"She said, '*Le chocolat et le lait . . . et la patience.*' I heard 'passion.' I think it needs cream . . . or butter."

"It doesn't."

"It needs something."

"She gave you the secret."

"Patience or passion?"

"Both. You have to stir it over a low flame for a long time."

"How long?"

"As long as it takes."

"How do you know that?"

"I don't know . . . but the low flame is important."

I stirred.

I was a witch stirring a cauldron. I was a maid beating the forbidden liquid to a froth for my mistress. I was a courtesan, preparing it for my lover. I was a child in my mother's kitchen.

I unleashed four dozen white balloons to float on the ceiling like bouquets of flying flowers, and lit as many candles. "*I* am the flame in my sadness," I said to myself. "I am the light in my darkness."

Soon the people I loved filled the shimmering room. Just before midnight, I poured the chocolate into champagne glasses and we climbed the rickety stairs to the roof, a glass in one hand, a white balloon in the other. When the sky exploded with joy, we drank the potion and sent the balloons soaring over the park into the fireworks.

I was in Paris, at Angelina, at four in the afternoon. This chocolate was as thick and as rich, but it had greater depth. It was an initiation, but not into night.

I was in Vienna, on the phone with my father for the last time. "How are you, Dad?"

"Fine. Fine. I have the feeling that something wonderful is going to happen before the year is out."

"Really? What?"

"I don't know."

"Is it going to happen to you?"

"Yes . . . and to you too."

I was in New York on New Year's Eve.

I let my balloon go. "Happy New Year,

Daddy." It flew into the air like a freed spirit. Someone started to sing. We all joined in, ragged at first. "Should auld acquaintance . . ."

"Happy New Year, Nathan."

"The chocolate is spectacular."

"It took forever."

"As long as it takes."

I drank — *we* drank — to patience, and passion. We said goodbye to the past, and we embraced the future, and each other, so warmly that unexpected tears came into my eyes. I tried to blink them away, but Nathan was whispering something in my ear. "Come to dinner tomorrow night and I'll buy you the Brooklyn Bridge."

BROOKLYN

Chapter 13

Brooklyn was a foreign country that night; only Manhattan was visible through the window. We sat down just as the sun was setting and the windowpanes in the glass castles were beginning to take its place.

"I wish I had a camera."

"You do," he said, taking a brand-new Nikon out of his jacket pocket. "The box wouldn't fit." He made a gesture to the view. "I know. You have cameras. I thought you needed a new one."

By the time I finished the roll, we were back in the black-and-white Manhattan of the thirties—the white lights of the black towers on the black river, under the achingly beautiful arc of the bridge. Seeing it laid out like a shimmering necklace had always stopped my heart; that night it started it again. I had arrived in the City of Light at last. This was the Dream City. This was Oz. Mecca. Jerusalem. Tuila.

I grinned at Nathan. "Someday, all this will be yours."

"Today."

I smiled, shy all of a sudden.

"What?" he said, almost able to read my expression.

"I can't remember what I felt about you when we were married . . . to them, I mean."

"What?"

"I can't remember. Did I want you?"

"I don't think so."

"Is your marriage over?"

"It was always over."

"How can you be sure?"

"I'm as sure as I can be."

"You're not divorced."

"Are *you*?"

I shook my head. He took one of my hands in both of his, touching me more deeply than all of the so-called love-making with all of the so-called men. I bent my head over the table and kissed his fingers. And smelled them. A sweet spiciness. A hint of darkness, but no danger.

"I always loved your hands."

An offer had been made, an offer I couldn't refuse. But in accepting it, I would be giving up all the other women's men. All the other men in the world. All the fairy tales on the shelf. My prince had come, and he wasn't a prince.

It wasn't the men I would miss; it was the longing.

I lifted my head to look at him, but there was something in the way. A bridge—a

structure of solid chocolate, with road-ways and walkways of *marquise*, *mousse*, and *ganache*. It stood in a river of *crème anglaise* against a cocoa-powder skyline. It was delirious—I took one bite—and delicious. I put my fork down.

"How do we know it won't be the same?"

"As what?"

"Our marriages. It looks the same."

"It doesn't smell the same."

"Here I am in another restaurant, eating another gorgeous chocolate thing…"

"With another Jew." He made me laugh, and he didn't make me cry. "I think what counts here is intent; it's the difference between murder and manslaughter. Are you in this for the chocolate?"

I didn't need to eat the Brooklyn Bridge; I needed to cross it.

"Does it feel the same?" he asked tenderly.

He was funny and sad and, yes, neurotic, but he was not afraid of my darkness, or my light. I looked far into his big, chocolate-brown, Brooklyn eyes, and I saw pools of love. I was being asked to dive deeper than ever before.

I never got what I longed for, so I could go on longing. Love was far more danger-ous. Love was real; it could be found and it could be lost.

But I had no choice. It was time to give up the boys

in the boybox for a man. There was no place left to go, except home.

Bittersweet home.

the CHOCOLATE

Chapter 2: New York

LI-LAC
Chocolate Fudge
120 Christopher Street
New York, NY 10014
TEL: 212-242-7374
FAX: 212-366-5874

FIFTH AVENUE CHOCOLATIER
Fresh Cream Truffles
510 Madison Avenue
New York, NY 10022
TEL: 212-935-5454
FAX: 718-361-8600

THE FOUR SEASONS
Chocolate Velvet
99 East 52nd Street
New York, NY 10022
TEL: 212-754-9494

POSTILION
Luscious Chocolate Sauce
Fond du Lac, WI
TEL: 414-896-0777
Available at: Dean & DeLuca

Chapter 3: Vienna

HOTEL SACHER
Sacher Torte
Philharmonikerstrasse 4
A-1010 Vienna
TEL: 011-43-1-514560
FAX: 011-43-1-51457-893
Will ship internationally

DEMEL
Trüffel Torte / Dorry Torte
Kohlmarkt 11
A-1010 Vienna
TEL: 011-43-1-536-1717

KM CAFÉ
Gerstner Torte
Kunsthistoriches Museum
Maria-Theresien-Platz
Burgring 5
1010 Vienna
TEL: 011-43-1-521770

GERSTNER
Gerstner Torte
Kartnerstrasse 15
1010 Vienna
TEL: 011-43-1-512-4963

SLUKA
Petits Fours
Rathausplatz 8
1010 Vienna
TEL: 011-43-1-427172

Chapter 5: Zurich

SPRUNGLI
Truffes du Jour
Paradeplatz
Bahnhofstrasse 21
8001 Zurich
TEL: 011-41-1-224-4646

HONOLD
Pavés Glacés
Rennweg 43
8001 Zurich
TEL: 011-41-1-211-5258

Chapter 6: Brussels

MANON
9a Chaussée de Louvain
1030 Brussels
TEL: 011-32-2-217-64-09

Also at: Bergdorf Goodman
754 Fifth Avenue at 58th Street
New York, NY 10022
TEL: 212-753-7300

MARY
73 Rue Royale
1000 Brussels
TEL: 011-32-2-217-45-00

WITTAMER
Place du Grand Sablon 12
1000 Brussels
TEL: 011-32-2-512-37-42
FAX: 011-32-2-512-52-09

Chapter 7: London

ROCOCO
House Truffles
Grand Cru Bars
321 Kings Road, Chelsea
London SW3 5EP
TEL: 011-44-171-352-5857
FAX: 011-44-171-352-7360

Chapter 8: Paris

ANGELINA
Chocolat à l'Africain
226 Rue de Rivoli
75001 Paris
TEL: 011-33-1-42-60-82-00
FAX: 011-33-1-43-44-82-35

MICHEL BELIN
4 Rue Docteur Camboulives
81000 Albi, France
TEL: 011-33-5-63-54-18-46
FAX: 011-33-5-63-54-07-12

9 Rue du Taur
31000 Toulouse, France
TEL: 011-33-6123-4021

MICHEL CHAUDUN
149 Rue de l'Université
75007 Paris
TEL: 011-33-1-47-53-74-40

CHRISTIAN CONSTANT
26 Rue du Bac
75007 Paris
TEL: 011-33-1-47-03-30-00

37 Rue d'Assas
75006 Paris
TEL: 011-33-1-45-48-45-51

JOEL DURAND
Place Jean de Renaud
13210 Saint Remy de
    Provence, France
TEL/FAX: 011-33-4-90-92-38-25

JEAN-PAUL HEVIN
3 Rue Vavin
75006 Paris
TEL: 011-33-1-43-54-09-85

16 Avenue de la Motte-Picquet
75007 Paris

LA MAISON DE
CHOCOLAT
52 Rue François Ier
75008 Paris
TEL: 011-33-1-42-27-39-44
FAX: 011-33-1-47-64-03-75

225 Rue Faubourg-St. Honoré
75008 Paris

8 Boulevard de la Madeleine
75009 Paris

19 Rue de Sèvres
75006 Paris

69 Avenue Raymond Poincaré
75116 Paris

25 East 73rd Street
New York, NY 10021
TEL: 212-744-7117
FAX: 212-744-7141

AU PALET D'OR
(ANDRÉ CORDEL)
136 Boulevard de la Rochelle
55000 Bar-le-Duc, France
TEL: 011-33-3-29-79-08-32
FAX: 011-33-3-29-79-20-70

LE ROUX
18 Rue du Port-Maria
56170 Quiberon, France
TEL: 011-33-2-97-50-06-83
FAX: 011-33-2-97-30-57-94

VALRHONA
26600 Tain-l'Hermitage,
France
TEL: 011-33-4-75-07-90-90
FAX: 011-33-4-75-08-05-17

LMC/VALRHONA
1901 Avenue of the Stars
Los Angeles, CA 90067
TEL: 310-277-0401
FAX: 310-277-4092

Available from:

Harry Wills
182 Duane Street
New York, NY 10013
TEL: 212-431-9731
FAX: 212-431-3620

Dean & Deluca
560 Broadway
New York NY 10012
TEL: 212-431-1691
FAX: 212-334-6183

Chapter 9: Walpole
BURDICK CHOCOLATES
Box 593
Walpole, NH 03608
TEL: 603-756-3701
TEL: 800-229-2419
FAX: 603-756-4326

Chapter 10:
The Big Island
HAWAIIAN VINTAGE
CHOCOLATE
4614 Kilauea Avenue, Suite 435
Honolulu, HI 96816
TEL: 808-735-8494
TEL: 800-429-6246
FAX: 808-735-9640

Also available from:
Continental Foods
TEL: 800-345-1543

Chapter 13: Brooklyn
THE RIVER CAFÉ
Marquise Brooklyn Bridge
1 Water Street
Brooklyn, NY 11201
TEL: 718-522-5200

the RECIPES

Chapter 1: Brooklyn

CHOCOLATE FUDGE

- *1⅓ cups firmly packed dark brown sugar*
- *1 cup white sugar*
- *pinch salt*
- *1 cup heavy cream*
- *1 stick unsalted butter, cut into squares*
- *3 ounces Nestlé's unsweetened chocolate, cut into pieces*
- *1 tablespoon vanilla extract*

1. Stir the sugars, the salt, and half the cream in a 2- to 3-quart saucepan until they blend. Place over low heat and stir until the sugar begins to dissolve and the mixture is warm.

2. Add the butter and chocolate and stir until they are both melted.

3. Heat until just before boiling and slowly add the rest of the cream while stirring.

4. Bring the heat up to medium and bring the mixture to a boil. Stir the boiling mixture while scraping bottom in the shape of a figure eight, for approximately 10 minutes.

5. Remove the pot from the stove and let the mixture cool until it is no longer hot when touched. Add the vanilla and beat for another ten minutes, or until the mixture begins to lose its sheen.

6. Pour or spoon into an 8-inch square pan. Even the surface with a table knife. When it cools, refrigerate until firm.

Yield: One pound of fudge.

ROMANIAN CHOCOLATE CAKE

THE CAKE

- *7 ounces European-style unsalted butter, softened*
- *½ cup water*
- *½ cup sifted unsweetened Dutch-process cocoa powder*
- *¾ cup sugar*
- *Grated zest of 1 lemon*
- *3 egg yolks*
- *3 egg whites*

1. Over a low flame, or in a double boiler, mix all the ingredients except the eggs, until the mixture is smooth. Transfer to a mixing bowl and beat in the egg yolks. Whip the egg whites until they form stiff peaks, and fold them carefully into the batter with a rubber spatula.

2. Pour the batter into an 8-inch square pan, lined on the bottom with wax or parchment paper and greased on the sides. Bake for 45 minutes at 375°F. The center will remain soft.

3. Cool the cake on a wire rack for 1 hour, and chill it for at least another hour.

4. When the cake is chilled, run a knife around the edges, put a large, flat plate on top, and, with one quick movement, flip the pan over, and shake hard, until the cake drops onto the plate. Spread the cream on the cake. Chill for another hour before serving.

THE CREAM

- *½ cup + 1 tablespoon sifted unsweetened Dutch-process cocoa powder*
- *½ cup sugar*
- *¼ cup water*
- *5 ounces European butter, softened*

1. Mix the cocoa powder and sugar in a bowl over simmering water, adding the water a little at a time until the sugar is completely dissolved and the mixture is smooth.

2. Take the bowl off the heat and beat in the butter, a little at a time, until the mixture becomes smooth again.

Yield: One 8-inch cake, enough for 8–12 servings.

Chapter 9: Walpole

CHOCOLATE TRUFFLES*

- ⅔ *cup heavy cream*
  (preferably not ultrapasteurized)

- *10 ounces finely chopped bittersweet chocolate*
  (with high cocoa content, preferably Valrhona
  Manjari, at 64 percent cocoa, or Valrhona
  Guanaja, at 70 percent cocoa)

- *2 ounces (4 tablespoons) unsalted butter*
  (preferably with low moisture content—
  a European butter or one made on a
  small farm), softened

- *8 ounces bittersweet chocolate*
  (preferably Manjari or Guanaja)

- *1 cup sifted unsweetened Dutch-process*
  cocoa powder (preferably Valrhona)

THE GANACHE

1. Bring the cream to a boil, and let it cool in a mixing bowl for a few minutes.

2. Add the chopped chocolate and whisk the pieces together gently.

3. Mix in the butter and pour the mixture into a flat pan. (If the pan is not made of stainless steel, line it with plastic film.)

4. After about four hours, put the mixture into a pastry bag and pipe out small dollops on a cookie tin or pastry board.

THE SHELLS

1. Melt the solid chocolate over low heat.

2. Dab the melted chocolate on the palms of your hands.

3. Pick up the dollops of *ganache* and roll them around in your hands until they are covered.

4. Pour the cocoa powder into a small tray or cake pan.

5. While the shells are still wet, set the truffles in the cocoa powder and push them around with a fork until they're covered. Let them dry on another tin or board.

Yield: About 50 truffles.

**Recipe courtesy of Burdick Chocolates.*

Chapter 12: New York

HOT CHOCOLATE*

- *2 cups milk*
- *72 pistoles Hawaiian Vintage Chocolate or 5 ounces Valhrona Manjari Chocolate*

1. Bring milk to a boil.

2. Turn the flame down low and add chocolate, stirring almost continually, until it becomes very thick. As long as it takes.

Yield: 2–4 servings.

*After Angelina.